CIGARETTE

The Catcher Series

BY JUDITH SWANSON

EDITED BY SHAMANDA OSBY

Cover by Monica Stanley

Happy Birthday

A stillness lingered over the silent room as the sun made its way into the dark space scattered about. It slowly lit up the corners, betraying dust particles and making them visible to the naked eye. The dead silence of the room was disturbed by the static of what may have been a recording player. Static blared from the metallic object as it swiftly and almost unnoticably zipped around the room. Suddenly, a tender yet, firm male voice filled the air as the object continued to fly. The voice softly sang, "Happy Birthday to you; Happy Birthday to you; Happy Birth-day dear Leon! Happy Birthday to you." There was a slight pause in the man's voice before he continued, "Son, I am so proud of you. You made it to another beautiful year. Look at my little man, **so** grown up. Make this day and year count. Be the man that I know you can be. There is nothing that you can't accomplish and don't let anyone tell you different." Then the recording stopped. The flying object finally came to a rest on the top of the nightstand. His actual alarm clock took over. "Good Morning, Sir! Happy Birthday, and, it's time to get up, UP, **UP**!"

The object lifted up again and hovered a few feet above a covered face. The sounds that it made echoed through the room. You could see that this was a clock that would be considered a relic by most because it was a much older model from the youth of its owner. This would be considered outdated for even his parents' era. Leon probably kept it this long because it always brought back memories of when his father use to teach him valuable lessons. The kind of lesson that a five year old needed to learn. His father believed that it was never too early to start. This was one of the fondest memories he had of his father. Fortunately, for him it was actually perceived within this gift. The initial shape created a perfect circle, as two miniature speakers sat neatly on top of it—resembling two perfectly circled ears. The clock appeared to resemble the character "Super Mouse", which was a popular cartoon character of his childhood. (He wasn't sure if it was still popular nowadays but he knew it had been in production for decades). This particular clock model predated his parents' generation. One would say that this model was quite primitive even during their time. They didn't have the capacity to be automated aside from making an annoying loud ring. Really, they couldn't even propel themselves around the room. Quite primitive indeed! Yet to Leon, the clock was simply a wonderful reminder of one of his happiest memories of his father. But that one night changed everything. "WHAT? Are you still in bed!" The clock shouted suddenly, pulling him from his memories, filling the air with its electronic voice. "It's your birthday. Time to get up and celebrate!" It continued and then went silent. "That's what you get for hitting the snooze button," he mumbled to himself. To no avail, he reached up and tried to grab the clock that flew around his face. He reached up for it a few more times before he finally caught the flying device. Once it was in his grasp he turned off the alarm as well as its propelling system.

From within the bed came a heavy sigh, he was anything but overjoyed for this day. Today was his 21st birthday, you would think one would be more joyful. Frightened by the thought of what this day held for him, he struggled to reopen his eyes and actually face his reality. He found more comfort within the darkness of his shut eyes than in the light of this day. Nonetheless, he slowly gave in to his awakening allowing the light to greet him. As he waited for his eyes to adjust, he tried to keep his focus on the chandelier above. It reflected the sun's light throughout the room. Like the clock, it was a relic from the past. The framing was silver and a circular pattern, within it were chrome pieces that created the illusion of a diamond pattern all the way around the surface. It provided a perfect reflection of the sun's light. Who would have thought that someone would see such a pretty sight on such a somber day? This was a somber day indeed despite the perfect reflection on the wall provided by the chandelier of perfectly shaped diamonds. In a failed attempt to delay the day, he rolled over to his other side giving him full view of the wall. 'If only there was another way to celebrate coming of age, instead of the tradition of facing "***The Catcher***", 'he thought to himself.

He realized that this was only one thing to do. Take the action he was reluctantly trying to delay. He simply changed his view to the blue-lined wallpaper which almost created the identical diamond shapes as the chandelier from ceiling to floor. Now he was looking out the open window which flooded the room with the day's light. As he gazed out of the window, he saw various sized blimps off in the distance. All he could make out from this distance were floating bubble but he knew what they were. It was obvious to him that these were airships going on their routine trips from one destination to another. He desperately wanted to be on one of them. Instantaneously, he envisioned himself on one of the larger ones that was a bit more visible. He could practically feel the plush seats underneath him as he stretched out his legs. The seats automatically adjusting to the length of his legs as he obsessed the stewardess conducting their duties ever so diligently. While the drones monitored the comfort of each passenger, allowing the stewardess to each one properly. The stewardess uniform was anything but conventional; the design was not proper but it still appealed to him just as well. The front of their dresses reached just above their knees and the backend barely above their ankles. A sudden honking from below quickly brought him back to reality, just as his mind drifted to a conversation he had with his best friend Greg. They'd decided to start his birthday celebration early and on this particular night the room was jammed packed with non-smokers enjoying a nightcap,gentlemen conversation and merriment. As they enjoyed their drinks, little drones flew around the room monitoring the intoxication level of each patron. Occasionally going back to the bartender informing them who cut off. The drones buzzed around a bit more furiously tonight due to the unusually large crowd. The crowd annoyed Leon a bit more than usual, which had him a little confused. It wasn't the first time that the lounge had been so crowded. They have been coming here since they were fifteen years old and have experienced many a crowded nights in this place. Despite this, he was utterly restless.

On this night, Leon and Greg sat at a round and well-polished cherry wood table placed at a comfortable distance from the bar. Leon passed his left hand over the table, allowing himself to enjoy the smoothness of the finished table top. As he took in the smoothness he was reminded of the glass partition that sectioned off the smoking area from the non-smoking area. His eyes fixated on the clear thick glass so hard that if he could he would have burned a hole right through it. On the other side were the ones that didn't mind or wasn't affected by the smoke - filled room as they enjoyed their drinks. "Would you fancy another drink?" Greg asked cheerfully. For the moment, he yearned for the ability to hold one of those toxic cigarettes between his lips to help ease his nerves since his drinks weren't doing the job. Even though he knew it would be the end of him. He seriously contemplated getting up and making his way to the other side of the partition. His allergies would not allow him to survive the encasement, let alone placing it between his lips. He even entertained the idea of entering that smoked-filled room and ending it all right then and there, not giving "the Catcher" a chance to provide its prediction. Just then Greg woke him from his thoughts by slamming his hand on the table and simply stated, "What are you worried about my dear man?" He mocked. He patiently waited for one of Leon's usual witty responses. When he didn't get any response he continued on in a manner that exhibited how intoxicated he truly was. As he spoke, he could barely remain seated in his chair. "There's only one thing you should be worried about....Oh! That's right there is nothing *TO* worry about. All except when it's going to happen but *then who cares.*" He placed his right hand on the table to help balance himself as he grabbed his drink with his left hand. He took a quick gulp and continued. "This gives you an excuse to have all the drinks you want and get piss ass drunk *on or before* your 21st birthday." Then he gave his friend the biggest grin, even the Cheshire cat would have been envious, before motioning him to drink more.

'WWWHHHHHHHY?' he screamed in his head bringing him back from his memory. As he returned to reality, he found himself staring up at the off white chipping ceiling paint which matched his feelings of hopelessness in his heart. His hair displayed his restlessness, as it was ruffled in every direction but the right one. It provided full view of his square face, which made him look more like a cartoon character from the old days. He worked very hard to maintain his baby smooth face, which only enhanced his cartoonist appearance. His pinstriped pajamas draped over his lanky slim body adding to his cartoonist sight. Unfortunately, there was nothing comical about this day for Leon. 'How can I get out of this?' he thought to himself as he searched frantically for a method out of his current situation. As he pondered how he could get out of his duty of the day, his watch suddenly began to make a loud cranking sound. A little excitement went through him as he heard the siren; this was his birthday gift to himself two weeks earlier. With all the different mobile devices out there, this was the latest and most up to date model. It was the only one that provided an audio and visual option, it was years ahead of its time compared to the rest. So like a good boy he got one for him and his mum, anything to help her stay relevant.

'Well I guess I don't have much of a choice now. I have to face ***this*** day.' He thought to himself as he reluctantly checked the identifier where it revealed that it was actually his mother calling him. 'At least she's in audio mode. Thank goodness! He realized that the technology was probably too advanced for her to comprehend and didn't remember how to put it into visual mode.' He really wasn't ready for anyone to see him in his current bedded state. How disheveled and depressed he would have looked to anyone who set eyes on him. Even through the communication device it would show. He let out a heavy sigh as he answered his watch, knowing full well if he didn't she wouldn't stop ringing him.

"Hel..." He barely got it out before he heard.

"LEON! Are you still in bed?" She screamed on the other side of the watch, in a manner that made you realize that she was making up for its compact size. She didn't even give him a chance to answer before screaming through the device again. "GET UP LEON!" She paused to catch her breath only to continue with, "Come on out and have breakfast with your mum on your *special birthday!*" He tried to answer her but all that came out was a groan. She paused for a moment longer waiting for him to try another attempt before she continued. "I'll be there in an hour. So you better get up!" He suddenly heard a high pitch tone followed by dead silence. He let out one last groan of surrender and finally made his way out of bed. For the first time since waking up he allowed his legs to dangle off the side for a few moments as he wished that there was a device that would assist him with delaying this day. After a few moments he gently jumped off his handcrafted redwood canopy bed. Good thing he had the foresight to lay out his clothes before venturing out with Greg the night before. He dug deep to find the motivation to actually start the day. Once he found the motivation he went running into the bathroom to bring his hair under control and have a quick shave; he grabbed his clothing and put them on as quickly. His attire consisted of a straight yet loose fitting crimson trousers, which imitated what most of the younger gentlemen are wearing these days. He carefully tucked in the white ruffled shirt that he chose to accompany his assemble. It laid fashionably well atop his crimson double-breasted vest. To complete his ensemble, he draped his Regency tailcoat over his shoulders. After a few turns and twist in front of his full length mirror, he was finally satisfied with the image that was gazing back at him. He did a quick flattening, tucking and adjusting just to be sure that he was presentable for the world out there. After he was completely satisfied with his grooming a smirk grew on his face. He was very happy at how smashing he looked. 'I'm really dashing!' he managed to think to himself, despite how dreary this day happen to be. This would have been the perfect attitude if this was a normal day of work for him as a Public Relations Representative. That's the positive attitude to have. Despite the dark cloud that loomed over this day, image was still everything. Being completely satisfied with his true presentation in the mirror, he turned and grabbed his gentleman's hat which was formed in a global shape. He carefully inspected it before placing it upon his head. He glanced into the mirror to assure that his appearance was still dashing. Finally, he grabbed his globe-top cane.

Within thirty-minutes of his mother's initial call his phone began to make its initial sound and vibrating. He was up, dressed and ready to go. Despite his mother telling him that she would arrive in an hour, he knew this wasn't so. His mother was never on time but she was always early. Just as he was finishing that thought and dusted off his hat he heard the insistent honking that came from his mother's vehicle below. 'Mum!' he thought to himself. She moves like clockwork. You can always depend on her.' He finished with a giggle. He then rushed over to his open window to catch a glance of his mother standing outside her vehicle with her left arm reaching into the carriage as she pressed the horn. As soon as he stepped into view at the window, his mother spotted him and immediately began waving frantically as a huge smile adorned on her face. Upon seeing the smile on her face he made a real attempt to appear as cheerful as possible for her. He knew that even from this distance that his mother's eyes would be able to detect the distress from her only child. Instead, he placed a huge smile on his face and waved joyfully at her.

Seeing her reminded him about the purpose of this dreaded day. He moved his eyes upward in efforts to catch sight of one of the flying vehicles from earlier one last time. Just to catch a glimpse of that fantasy of running away once again before heading down. Unfortunately for him they were all out of view. His eyes did happen to fall upon a billboard that displayed an advert for Nicline, located on top of the building across the street. The advert was quite simple; it didn't mimic the fancy animated billboards. Instead it simply showed a bottle adorning a Nicline label. To the right it had the wordings "Nicline, your cure to tobacco and nicotine allergies." His mind was drawn back down to the street where he caught sight of two gentlemen dressed in tailcoats and top hats. Indicating that they were gentlemen of privilege. The two men were attempting to make their way across the street when a puff of smoke escaped the cigarettes that they were smoking. The puff of smoke made its way up the sky as one of the gentlemen made an attempt to check his watch as they crossed the street. Suddenly, Leon realized that he almost forgot a critical part of his daily morning routine. He neglected to take his dosage of Nicline. 'I would hate to drop dead before I actually meet with the Catcher.' he sarcastically thought to himself .He reached over to his dresser like his life depended on it. Which it actually did! He reached over and grabbed a bottle that was identical to the bottle from the advert. Once he had the bottle in hand he carefully twisted off the dropper and nervously eyeballed a measurement. Satisfied with the measurement, he shakily placed the dropper right above his tongue and squeezed the contents onto it. After making a face of utter disgust, he repealed the bottle and placed it into the inner pocket of his outer jacket. Double-checking that he hadn't forgotten anything else he made his way down to meet with his mother. Before closing the door to his studio apartment, he turned to take one last look around. His glance was quite dramatic as if this was the last time he would see his place of residence again. This actual apartment was part of a complex series for single men along this block. This was the designated residence for men going from single-hood to a life of matrimony. Ironically, these residence had an age limit of twenty-five years, the standard age for entering matrimony. Should a young man surpass the age limit of such residence, he is gracefully relocated to the residence allocated for single men above the age of twenty-five. They are also placed in a government funded matchmaking service. This seemingly was not a concern for Leon due to his current age of twenty-one. He felt that he had enough time to reach this goal despite the more pressing issues of this particular day.

As he made his way onto the street, Leon appeared to be

refreshed and ready to take on the world. As the saddness within his heart said anything but, as he stepped out through the outer doors, he could see traffic was minimal, which wasn't uncommon during the mid-morning hours. Most of the buildings in this area were identical to the one that Leon lived in, except for one or two, which were designated for family housing. He also noticed that the ground levels of the buildings were completed with different shops that catered to the daily needs of the local residence. He finally caught sight of his mother and silently took in her attire as he made his way to her. There was no way that he could miss her crimson rich skirt, which flowed like a river with the slightest movements. The skirt touched the ground not exposing her ankles and it didn't puff out like the younger ladies wore nowadays. It was a bit more conservative but flowed when she moved all the same. The black blouse that she wore gently laid on top of the upper part of her skirt ever so neatly. To compliment her entire ensemble, she pulled her hair back into a tidy bun. Yet, this was to plain for her. She topped everything off with a miniature top hat which tilted to the right side of her head. It appeared that her smile had gotten wider as he approached her, which he really didn't think was possible. Once he was close enough for his mother to hear him, he mumbled something that sounded similar to, "Morning,

Mum!" As soon as he was within her reach, she threw her arms around him quickly and tightly as she cheered, "Happy Birthday, Sweetie! You're *finally* 21." She made no effort to be discreet about her excitement or his age. She made so much of a commotion that within seconds they were being circled by one of the many peacekeeping droids that patrolled the city streets. This metallic sphere made a few rounds around them before coming to a sudden stop and its sides opened up. As quickly as it opened, a stream of red and blue light exited and scanned the area; specifically Leon and his mother. This was a normal occurrence whenever his mother was around. Once the drone was satisfied that there were no civil disobedience going on it went on his way. While the drone was conducting its check for peace, Leon's mother's words fell upon the ears of a few passer-byers. One or two stopped in their tracks trying to comprehend the joy in her voice, causing one person to almost trip. The remaining patrons simply glanced with sadness in their eyes; they knew the cost of becoming twenty-one in these days. He heard a passerby mention, "Poor mate! Not a good day for him at all." A set of gentlemen walked past them completely unaware of the conversation that had been exchanged between Leon and his mother. As they passed by they let out a huge puff of smoke that made its way between Leon and his mother. A look of concern came over her cheerful face as she watched the smoke slowly move between them. The smoke appeared to stop and linger right in front of Leon's face for a few extra moments before it continued its ascension to the sky above. When he didn't have a reaction she became more relaxed. "Glad to see that you took your elixir!" she stated. His mother was completely relieved that her baby boy was actually acting like an adult. He had taken his elixir, which meant that he was actually taking his condition more seriously. She was so moved that her eyes started to become misty with emotion.

Once his mother finally released him from her dramatic hug, she didn't give him a chance to react. As quickly as she released him, she just as quickly grabbed his hand and literally dragged him to the other side of the vehicle. To his amazement she moved ever so quickly and gracefully with her attire. As she shoved him into her antique model car, he couldn't help but wonder why she held on to it. Most of the cars these days looked nothing like her vehicle an old stage coach from ancient and uncivilized days. Back in those days they didn't have the convenience of the mechanical advancements of today. They couldn't even move those vehicles on their own. They were actually pulled along by horses.

Horses!?! Luckily, his mother's vehicle didn't require the assistance of horses to move from place to place. The only benefits that he could think of was that nowadays was that the driver rode inside the actual vehicle instead of outside and on top of it. Also that it wasn't drawn by horses. In the front left side, one had the ability to control it easier. As soon as they climbed into it the driver had the steering wheel before them. To the right was an adjustment for the perfect leg room for whoever sat in the driver's seat. Between the two front seats laid the shifting mechanism, which came up thru the floor of the vehicle. It was a simple rod that allowed the driver to shift gears. It came up high enough for the driver to reach it effortlessly. This particular vehicle had seats that was covered with hand-crafted black leather, to provide maximum comfort for anyone that had the pleasure of sitting in them.   For anyone else that rode in the vehicle the back had two rows of seats. The first set of seats were directly behind the driver, causing the rider to face the opposite direction. Providing them the full view of the rear window. The second set was facing the same forward direction as the driver.

She didn't waste any time shoving Leon into the vehicle, for her the boy could never move quickly enough.   Once he was actually in the vehicle, she swiftly moved to the driver's side and jumped in. The vehicle was started and they were on their way before he had a chance to even close his door. Yet as they started on their way his face began to turn green. Aware of his sudden physical anxiousness, he began to search his memory for any experience that could have been worse than this situation. As he quickly scanned his brain he couldn't immediately come up with anything. Mostly due to his nervousness with his mother's driving. His mother was filled with too much joy to actually take notice of her son's change of facial color. She was all too happy to spend a day with her son. While his mother was all too happy to proceed with this day, Leon himself felt as if they were enroute to his very own funeral. For some it was close enough. He began to feel anxious as he stared into the distance. He drifted off again trying to think of any way to escape his current predicament. Unfortunately, his mind went to an even darker place. He must've been at least fourteen years old wearing a suit that was more uncomfortable than not. The room was filled with several men and women dressed in all black. 'No this is not where I want to be,' he thought to himself, as he was pulled deep into his past. Much further than he intended to go. In this memory his eyes appeared to be closed initially, once he opened them he was greeted with a gentle face of a man adorning a curled up mustache. The mustache sat atop a very warm smile.

“How is my sleepy birthday boy?” he asked. The feelings of back then and now began to merge as one. Instant joy started to fill his every being. He couldn’t contain the smile that suddenly emerged on his face. This was a worthwhile memory for him. His father was so creative with each of his birthdays. He always took special care to make sure each birthday was extra special. He couldn’t help but to wonder if his father was trying to take into account that he suspected that he wouldn’t be here on this very important birthday. His mother broke his concentration, "Well! Aren't you going to ask me?" she asked as she happily drove. His mother’s smile never faltered. A more modern vehicle would make for a smoother ride. He couldn’t bare her cheeriness anymore so he looked out his window and tried to look up at the sky but his eye caught another advertisement that answered his mother’s question. It brought him back to his childhood and more happier times.

He giggled to himself as he tried to pluck the memory of the tellie advertisement from his mind. He barely caught his mother’s words when he finally turned to her and gave her a look (the look a teenager would give a parent that wasn't completely in touch with the modern day happenings). "What am I supposed to ask?" He was reluctant to ask that question but couldn’t resist. As soon as he did the one thing he thought couldn’t occur did. Her smile got even wider. "Aren't you going to ask me where I'm taking you for your very special birthday?" She responded as if she was teasing a toddler with his birthday gift. Just then the memory came to him.

International Pancake Emporium

Leon’s mind drifted to when he was about seven years old. He was sitting with his favorite Super Mouse toy in hand while he watched the latest episode on the tellie that his father had just purchased. As the screen faded to commercial, an image appeared on the screen simply stating “***International Pancake Emporium***” in nice large letters. After a few moments the jingle filled the room as it escaped the tellie.

♪When you’re feeling hungry

And in need to celebrate. ♪

♪Come on over to the Emporium

And have yourself a treat.♪

As the jingle continued to fill the room an image popped up that caused Leon’s little mouth to water. This is despite the fact that his little belly was already filled with a wonderful homemade breakfast prepared by his father. His father made him bacon, eggs and the fluffiest muffins. Like any child that has just set eyes on the most precious toy that they have set eyes on. His eyes widen as wide as they can get, as he watched images of various types of pancakes displayed on a nicely polish table. The jingle continued on as the picture slowly moved across the table.

♪If you don't find your desire,

You can make your own.♪

On the other side of the table, the camera stopped on the joyful face of a child about the same age of little Leon. He was joyfully holding a knife and fork as his face glowed in wonderment. He licked his lips with great enthusiasm. It took the child a few moments to move his eyes from the appeals delicious treats before him and realized that the camera was focused on him. Just when you thought his grin couldn't get any bigger - it did! He sat straight up and adorned a grin from ear to ear. The screen started to fade from the young boy's joyful face to a smaller table with a plate in the center of the triple decker pancake. It was topped with strawberry syrup with shocks of strawberries. On top of that was sprinkled a good amount of chocolate chip. The young child jump into a seat at the table. He pulled the plate closer and began to immediately dig into the delectable dish. As he ate he couldn't stop himself from dancing in his seat. The view widened to show the aisle right next to the table. Suddenly a group of the waite staff appeared and broke out into a group dance. One of the dancing staff stuck out their hand to the young child as an invitation for him to join them. He joined in. With him occasionally running back to the table to take a bite from his pancakes.

♪For a great experience,
Just come to the Emporium♪

As they continued to dance an image of the store front faded in, with more members of the staff standing in the store front. Above them was the typical ***INTERNATIONAL PANCAKE EMPORIUM*** awning. All with smiles on their faces as they sang the last line.

♪Come to the International Pancake Emporium.♪

As the image faded to black in front of the young Leon, so did the memory from the older Leon. As the memory faded he found himself back in the vehicle with his mother, on his 21st birthday.

Breakfast with Mum

As the memory faded from his mind, he cringed as her words came to the forefront. His eyes never left the view of sky, after a few moments he let out a heavy sigh. He realized that he had no choice but to answer his mother. He simply stated, "Mum, you're taking me to where you take me every birthday! We're going to the International Pancake Emporium." He sang the last sentence of the jingle in a sarcastically tone, almost to the tune of the advertisement. As soon as that last note escaped his lips, his mind threw him back to his younger years once again. To a time within this very vehicle. He was about nine years old; his mother was driving like she always did and his father was in the passenger seat. The three of them happily sang the theme song for IPE as a very youthful Leon bounced excitedly in the backseat. If anyone was permitted to attend this trios impromptu concert, they would think that Leon and his father were competing to see who could sing the loudest and off key. In the meantime, his mother tried her hardest to actually maintain the melody. For the young Leon it was absolutely the best place to go, especially for their antics. He truly enjoyed how the staff would randomly break out into song and dance. While they genuinely encouraged the children to join in. If you weren't into their dancing, you could always become mesmerized by the uniqueness of the staff's uniform and their display of the latest new gadgets. You could never find any of the wait staff wearing the same uniform. They wore the signature uniforms from different countries and profession. This memory brought him back to his earlier fantasy about the stewardess uniform. Despite the fact that he could not recall ever seeing that design there, he couldn't help but to wonder if he ever did see that particular uniform there. After a patron was done being amazed at the waite staff and their antics, they would have a chance to be captivated by the decorations on the wall. There were flags from every friendly nation around the world as well as photographs and paintings of key points in history. There were also plaques in different languages all saying the same thing '*Welcome to the International Pancake Emporium.*' It was easy to fall in love with this place because they were so inventive with the way they presented their delicious selection. At least through the eyes of a child. Back then he was very fond of one of their famous signature pancake called 'The Chocolate, Chocolate Chip Deluxe'. The memory alone caused a grown up Leon's mouth to water. To add to memory of this particular dish, he could clearly see the lightly brown pancake. The color provided the proof of the special chocolate ingredient that was added into the batter. Throughout the stacks of pancakes peeked little hints of chocolate chips here and there? Strategically placed on top were more chocolate chips to create various facial expressions accompanied with whip cream for good measure. Despite the fact that he had found his favorite dish, he was quite fond of their many unique creations. Within his mind he could see and smell the yellowery, sweet 'Banana Bonanza Buddy pancake', or the gooey goodness of the 'Strawberry Dandy Supreme' pancake. Better yet the wonderfully sweet 'Lavish Licorice' and the list can go on and on. Their selection brought wonderment to everyone, young and old. Leon's mouth began to water again as he remembered the different combination.

Yet, for Leon, today was not the day for such a happy place, not even the tune from the tellie would be amusing enough to bring a true smile to his face. "And we're going to have a *very special birthday pancake breakfast*," he added with as much sarcasm that he could muster. For the first time since he met up with her a frown formed on her face as she let out a weighted sigh but then her smile returned to her face immediately.

"I'm **NOT** taking you to the IPE" she sang in her normal cheerful manner. "Since today is a particularly ***special*** birthday, I decided to take you to a more fitting and ***adult*** place for this day. It's a nice quiet little diner that I know of. Befitting of your new mature age."

'A diner!' he thought. He paused for a few moments, trying to make sense of his mother's sudden change of routine and choice. If there was anything that was true about his mother is that she was truly a creature of habit. It was strictly against her nature to deviate from her routine, especially when it came to the annual celebration of her son's birthday. It was especially odd for her selection for a replacement. Her choice for a diner appeared to be nothing but an act of desperation. Her way of trying to provide him some sort of comfort for what the day actually held ahead. Even he was completely confused how she came to the conclusion that this would make him feel better about this day. Maybe she thought this would make him feel better about the events that were to come, yet not even this change would make this day better. It actually felt more like a downgrade of the day. A diner was somewhere you went when there is no place else to go after an insane night with your best mate. Usually, after one of those insane nights at the gentlemen club filled with nothing more than drinking and boyish play. If that isn't the case it would be the place you go when you get a late night hunger gnawing within your stomach and the local eateries are closed or even when your night didn't quite go as planned. Especially, when you want to be left alone and really not in the mind set to deal with anyone else or the world for that matter. Their bots weren't ever up to date and in less than optimum service. This was the last place that would come to mind when contemplating a place to have one's birthday celebration, unless you were a renegade or a delinquent. Yet, after some thought, he realized that on this particular birthday he was not in the mood to deal with others or even celebrate. So the choice was an appropriate one. There was nothing he could do but resign himself to this trip. Besides he WAS in the passenger seat. He took a deep breath before he finally asked, "Alright mum, I'll bite," he finally stated. "I just have to know. What is so special about this particular diner? Are their pancakes ultimately the best in the world? *Better than IPE's*? "He ended with an obvious sarcastic tone, just enough not to show her any disrespect.

She completely disregarded his sarcastic tone as she let out another heavy sigh. She finally provided a hint of acknowledgment of the events that were to take place today. "On such a day like today, you would question…" her emotions were starting to get ahead of her. She took a moment to gather herself. "I just thought that we could do something a little different to break up the mood." Slowly the smile that appeared to be permanently pasted on her face, slowly faded away. There was no need to have a mood decipher handy to know that her mood had become uncomfortable for her. Her eyes went completely blank as if she got lost within some inner dialog. After a few moments of silence, she suddenly woke from her daze. She managed to gather herself. "What?" she barked as if responding to an unspoken objection. "I'm not allowed to change our routine a little?" Her aggressive tone began to ease when she realized her outburst was directed at her son. The look of shock came over his face once he released that his mother's smile didn't return. There were very few times that his mum addressed him with such a tone, never for such a minor infraction and never in his adult life. He sat straight up. He would have stood up if it wasn't for the fact that he was in a moving vehicle and the agitated person was at the wheel. His reaction caused her to realize how dramatic she was being. She recomposed herself and returned to her original cheerful demeanor. Her smile quickly returned as she spoke. "I just thought we would do something different since you're finally 21," she took a moment before continuing. "Also, since you're legal now, I wanted to share my son's first ***legal*** drink with him, just to see if you can hold your own with this old lady." She giggled a little trying to lighten up the mood, unsure if it was for him or herself. "We both know that the IPE doesn't provide beverages that appeal to the mature palette, so I had to find another place." She finished in a matter of fact tone. With that a smile grew onto Leon's face, before he realized it he fell into a giggle fit. No matter the situation, she could never cease to surprise him on how far she would go just to make him feel loved.

"Thanks Mum!" He managed among his giggles.

For the remainder of the ride they only discussed pleasant topics. They discussed everything under the sun, everything except the events that were before them. Despite the fact that most of the topics were mindless in nature, they did a great job to keep the mood light. They discussed the latest state of the recent war to the latest government conspiracy theories that they'd recently heard. He even engaged with her about her favorite tellie-series. He listened ever so attentively to her update, despite the fact he really didn't care for the show. Now and then they would revisit a fond memory of his earlier birthdays. The majority of them took place at the IPE and involved a dancing Leon. His mother recalled one event in particular that did not take place at the IPE; it was a time when a young Leon made on attempt to fly off the roof of the house as he used to watch his favorite cartoon character do. She burst into laughter as she remembered that Super Mouse outfit he had created, she could barely get the memory out from her lips. "Do you remember the time you grabbed your light blue pajamas and your red undergarment?" she giggled to herself before she could continue. "You threw those pajamas on and those red things right over them. You ran into the closet and grabbed your red bathrobe and headed to the roof saying 'Super Mouse to the rescue!'" she laughed a bit. "And your...," she stopped short of mentioning his father's reaction to the entire ordeal. They were trying so hard to keep away from anything that would bring that pain to either of their hearts. They both had their memories of him but rarely did they speak of them or him for that matter. Especially with the Catcher waiting for them. Within all their discussions not once did she mention or even hint about the Catcher and the daunting task that awaited them. It was actually starting to feel like a real outing with his mother with no other pretense but to enjoy the day and celebrate his birthday.

Leave it to his mum to make everything all better. He was quite amazed at her ability to sit there and talk about nothing and yet everything under the sun all at once. All with that smile on her face, some would say it was permanently stuck on her face. This was one of the most enjoyable visits he has had with his mum in a long time. He almost forgot the reason for this enjoyable yet bumpy ride. Eventually they arrived at the diner where she immediately made her way to the back to park. This disappointed him because it really didn't give him a chance to see the architecture of the actual building, which was the only appeal that the place had from what he could see. This wasn't a part of town that he frequented so he really couldn't recall this particular place. They made their way to the entrance as he tried to figure out the significance of THIS diner, it didn't appear all that special. Little did he realize that this diner was right next to one of many of the most avoided place in the country, the Future Center. He was completely unaware that his mandatory appointment was only steps away, thanks to the maneuvering of his brilliant mother. For a brief moment, Leon remembered that it was his birthday and actually started to get excited, until he realized what today actually meant. Just then that sinking feeling started to come back, and his birthday joy was short lived. There wasn't enough alcohol in that entire diner to help calm his nerves but it was worth trying. 'I hope my

Mum is ready to get me smashingly happy' he thought to himself. "That's basically what it's going to take for me to get through this day," he mumbled under his breath. "What was that dear?" she inquired as she barely caught his words. He didn't want to ruin this outing for her. She took extra care and thought to try to put him at ease. So he simply replied, "Nothing! It was nothing. Let's go inside so we can enjoy my very special birthday breakfast." And flashed her a smile.

He made his way out of the car and they walked into the diner. From the moment he walked in he could tell that the floor plan was in the form of an 'L'. The place was semi-filled with various characters that could have appeared from any random cartoon show to a melodramatic tragic film. The walls were covered with pictures and paintings depicting key moments within the development of the country's history, even of the failed rebellion of 73. Yet, these inspiring, and uplifting pictures only added to the gloomy feeling. The oddest part was although the windows were wide open and shadeless, the dark mood appeared to keep the light at bay. Not to mention the attire of the majority of the patrons.

He noticed that a few of the women were actually wearing trousers, which happen to be the latest trend. It appeared odd because the only real women who wore trousers were usually in a jungle somewhere proving that they were just as capable as men in the art of exploring. This was not a trend that Leon was very fond of at all. He didn't find anything appealing about it. A few of them looked as if they haven't laid their heads to rest in several days. The other patrons were dressed in very dark and odd clothing's that really didn't seem fit to be worn in public. He also noticed a few of the females wore skirts that exposed their ankles, which was a trend among those that were anti-establishment. The men were in no better condition; one appeared to forget his shirt and his outer jacket as his inner vest remained unbuttoned. There were only four staff working, all dressed in gray and dreary uniforms. The women wore skirts that dragged on the floor, showing no pleats or imagination of design of any kind. Their blouses were just as plain, simple, pressed and form fitted. The men wore shirts of the same accompanied with straight legged trousers, just like the skirts no pleats or design. The uniforms matched the mood of this place perfectly. Depressing! None as elegantly dressed as Leon and his mother or as cheery and smiling as they were either- the after effect of their joyful ride. Leon tried to take everything in as they were being seated in a quiet corner that appeared to be prepared just for them to celebrate this special day. His mother ordered their first round of Jack Daniels, his first "LEGAL" drink was shared with his mother, just as she had wished. Who would've thought? That Daniels Whiskey actually helped him relax much to his surprise. He really wasn't sure if it was his yearning to escape or just the fact that he was actually enjoying THIS moment.

From the moment they stepped into the diner, his mind was completely pre-occupied with becoming intoxicated, not even the Catcher distracted him from this goal. In fact, that was the motivation for his growing urge. He wanted to it so much so that he hadn't notice his mum was hanging with him shot for shot. It wasn't until he made an attempt to have a giggle with her did he realize that she was a bit off. It wasn't the fact that he has never seen her drunk before, she has always grabbed a few drinks here and there at social events but never to ***this*** extent. For the first time, in such a long time, he saw a glimmer of sadness in her eyes. A truly deep sadness, he paused as he was taken aback by the deep growing sadness within her eyes. It was so deep that it caused his heart to ping in pain just a bit. The sadness appeared to almost overwhelm her to the point where she nearly began to cry. Had he not been sitting there she probably would. It has been such a long time since he saw tears rolled from his mum's eyes.

That day returned to him as if it had just occurred yesterday. It was such a horrific day for both of them. There was no denying the pain and agony that showed within her eyes. Anyone else would have screamed out in pain but she didn't. She wouldn't. She just let the sadness in her eyes look over the dreadful ambiance of the diner as it blended in. Leon took a quick look around the diner to see if anyone noticed the change in his mother's mood, it was at this moment that he saw it's true dreary appearance. To add to the creepy and unshakable chill that this place provided, the patrons themselves were drably dressed in dark and morbid clothing. Now that he was seated, he had the opportunity take a good look at the place and its occupants. He realized that the mood reminded him of one of his worst memories in his life. One that both he and his mother shared, the one that brought the sadness to her eyes. He couldn't stop himself from going back there as he took a careful look around and ended back within his mother's eyes. She didn't react when the tears began to stream down her face as she stood by her husband's casket, refusing to say her final goodbye on principal alone. That day he didn't just bury his father and she didn't just bury her husband. A piece of their heart and soul was ripped from their very being and covered with dirt. A very young Leon did everything he could to keep a stiff upper lip and be strong for her. He really didn't want to be here - this memory was too much for him to bear. It took every ounce of his energy to remove himself from this awful memory and found himself staring back into his mother's sad eyes once again. Even the sight of her was too much for him to bear. He moved his focus from her eyes to her entire face. Then he realized a seriousness that wasn't there before. This was odd for him because ever since his father's funeral he couldn't truly remember seeing so much as a frown on her face before earlier today. She woke up from her own inner thoughts when she noticed that he has become aware of her distress. Her mind seemed to be in a more agonizing place than his because she suddenly grabbed his hands in such a dramatic manner and her face changed into a softer and apologetic manner before she said, "Oh, Sweetie! This is not how we thought it would be. How any of us thought..." Her words completely confused him, he was unsure if they were continuing a conversation that he was not aware of before this point. For a moment, he thought that maybe he was so caught up in his own thoughts of despair that he missed the beginning of the discussion they were supposed to have or perhaps she forgot to verbalize her own inner thoughts. The look of confusion on his face made her realized that she was reacting to her own inner dialog. She took a moment to regroup her thoughts before explaining to him in a calmer tone. "When they came up with the concept of the CK730, it was supposed to be the best thing for everyone." She paused to catch her breathe. *"For mankind."* She took another moment. *"For our salvation.* It was supposed to help us **prepare** for the inevitable." It was as if she was pleading with him, as she rang her hands in a symbolic way of washing them clean. She then reached into her purse to pull out a handkerchief to wipe the sweat from her brow unaware of the tears that were falling. After a few moments, she continued, "I mean it helped with your father's passing. Sort of!" She paused. "When it happened, it made, it ..." she took a breath. "It was supposed to be...easier. Then again there is no easy way to face death."

She paused, again, and, smiled a little as the memories of her long gone love, who was taken away way too soon started to return. Her memory forced her back to a time when Leon was about five years old. He was on a swing that hung from the tree in their backyard just an odd tradition but fun nonetheless. The sun slipped through the branches and leaves, shining on the smiling face of her husband as he pushed a joyful Leon. That smile would bring such brightness to any situation. She thought to herself, she could really use that smile today. Not within her memories but in the flesh and blood. She would have given anything to have him there right now with that smile of his, oh! How he could better deal with these type of situations so much better than her. Before she could drift completely into her memory she quickly returned back to the diner and to her son, the son that needed her right now. She let out a heavy sigh before continuing her comment. "We were prepared because of the machine. We had everything in place for that day. More importantly we were able to enjoy every moment with him. ***Every moment.***"

After that sentence, she drifted back to one of her most precious memories. Her hair was matted down with sweat and resembled the worst representation of a bird's nest. She lied in a hospital bed as the look of exhaustion took over her entire physical body. As she tried to catch her breath and take everything in, just then a nurse escorted her husband into the room. He was so excited that he ran to her bedside with that big old smile on his face as she handed him the tiny bundle that was Leon, freshly born. Tears of joy ran down her face as she looked upon his son for the first time. She began to remember the joy she felt and the joy in his face but then quickly brought herself back by the realization of the day. Leon was about 10 or 11 when it became mandatory to face the CK 730, to him this has always been the way. "Yes, it's true! We didn't know at the time or the place but we knew the how. It was because we knew the how; we were able to live our lives accordingly, to avoid whatever it was at all cost. Well as much as one can avoid death. But today...." She paused and wiped away another tear that happened to escape her unaware that this wasn't the first. She took a deep breath and continued, "Today has brought to me the realization of how truly selfish we were by wanting the CK730 to even exist. I remember... "

She paused as she had actually and finally named the elephant in the room. She gathered herself before she continued. "I remember when 21," she paused again to catch her breath, "turning 21 was the best thing in the world. Back then you couldn't wait until your 21st birthday when you could have that first ***legal*** drink with your friends and get ever so smashed. So smashed that they had to carry you home or you spent the night in the slammer..." She let out a giggle as she smiled before she continued. "But it was more of a rite of passage. But this machine we wanted oh..." She paused again to catch her frustrated breath. "Oh, so much! We had no idea we were taking away the joy of turning 21 from our children. We never saw this coming. There was no way we could know..." She paused to take a breath before she continued. "I'm so upset they made it mandatory, and I'm more upset that you... my baby have to go through this. I regret that you don't know a life before the Catcher. But I can honestly say – and you will know this after you come out of that room. You have to know; you DO have time to live your life. Time to meet that special woman," she thoughtfully paused, "or man. It's hard to tell what you kids are into nowadays." She smirked at him hoping to bring a little humor to his heart before she returned to her serious demeanor. "You can still have a child," she stopped to find the words," **no matter which way you go at it.** Whatever you do, don't forget to love them as much as I have and still love you. So..." she stopped as the waiter returned. She asked for one more shot and a cup of tea. After the waiter left to complete the request she continued. "Love them and raise them with the love and patience that your father had for you." Leon opened his mouth to react but he didn't have a chance because the waiter returned with his mother's request. He placed both drinks in front her and continued on his way. She quickly took the shot and placed it in front of him. This shot was truly his birthday shot because it was the only one he was to take on his own at least as far as his mum was aware. His true birthday shot, so was the new tradition for one's twenty-first birthday within the age of The Catcher. She grabbed the cup and actually toasted as she looked at her son and said with the most joy she had since she started their conversation. "Have this shot and know you have the rest of your life to live."

Leon was truly touched by his mother's words. A feeling of shame came over him for almost allowing his dread and resentment ruin this special moment with her. He knew the history of the machine and was quite aware that The Catcher emerged from his parents' generation; it was part of their history. He was quite aware of their hopes and understood that their hearts were in the right place. Yet when the government gets involved, dreams and hopes are thrown out the window and the agenda of those in power takes over. Which no one has ever really figured out what that could be! He grabbed that shot that his mother had placed before him and downed it as if he was out with his mates after they have dared him or something like that. After placing the shot glass in front of him, he waved the waiter over and ordered a cup of tea. The waiter quickly brought him the cup and he joined his mother who was sipping her cup slowly, as if she was waiting for him to catch up to her. Until his first sip of tea, he didn't realize how tipsy he had truly become. He really needed to regroup so he didn't fuss as they prepared

for what was coming next.

Civic Duty

The tellie in the diner came on with a clicking noise emerge from the screen. It is immediately followed by a crackly sound right before thousands of white dots started to dance on the screen. As if queuing the image to change, the crackling seemed to lessen as the white dots followed suit. As the image fades details of another image emerged giving way to a clear view, allowing you to see a space about foot apart between each bar. As the image becomes clearer you can see a replica of the sun perfectly centered on the gate. The sun itself had a sunshiny smile on it accompanied with the dimpled cheeks. Once the camera was done focusing on the top of the gate, it refocuses to show what appears to be at first a series of warehouses. The buildings had no windows but on a few you could see hints of closed cargo doors, giving you a peek into the elegant and prestigious filming facility known as The Sunshine Studios. This is the birthplace of many cutting edge films of the day. As the camera pans over the entire area, it added to the feeling of enjoyment, as this feeling begins to settle in, a voice comes from beyond the scene and states "***Welcome to the time of elegance and scientific wonder.*** "

As soon as the word "scientific" is mentioned a scene begins to fade in displaying a typical data room. The wall that surrounded the lab was hidden behind large metal machines that were the typical metallic color with each machine being covered with blinking colorful lights. From time to time an electrical beeping sound would escape from them and fill the room with their functionality. The space that wasn't occupied by machines had men and women in lab coats that bustled around the room. Some carried trays filled with test tubes in their hands filled with multicolored liquid, while others simply carried clipboards occasional stopping in front of a machine and took a few notes. The voice came over again saying, "***We have the pleasure of all the wonderful comforts, enjoyments and advancements of this world. All this has been made possible by the selfless sacrifice of those serving on the front line.***"

Suddenly the sound of bombing erupts from the screen, an image appears to come closer into view until you are able to see the front line of the current conflict come into view. As the scene gets closer you are able to get a clear view of a trench as soldiers race back and forth within it, with their weapons in hand. As the soldiers are rushing about, you see one or two personnel in the same uniform. Instead of running like the rest, they stood around barking orders. From here and there one or two of the running soldiers would stop for a moment to catch the orders before racing off quickly to follow them, it would appear. Occasionally, dust would fly up in the air as a result of some type of ordinance. It's during this time the voice returns. "***This is a wonderful example of civic duty and patriotic pride. Doesn't it make you PROUD of our men in uniform.***" The image disappears and gives way to the dancing white dots once again. When the voice continues, "***The constant improvements and developments of our technology has helped us make our lives and country a more civilized place to live in.***"

From the white snow another scene fades in showing a very elegant and highly decorated dining room. As one tries to take in the entire beauty of this image, your eyes are forced above the table. There you find a chandelier that is perfectly centered, high above the room. The exterior framing of the chandelier was silver in color. The design was almost completely circular, allowing one to see the pattern that was within this sphere. As you look a bit closer at the design you can see the chrome pieces that created the illusion of a light of diamonds on all the surface that the light touches. Where they should have been a hole for the diamond a clear crystal piece was placed there, perfectly representing a diamond with an electrical bulb to illuminate a light. Directly below the chandelier was the large dining table that initially caught your attention, filled with every elegant type of food. There was enough food on that table to feed many mouths. Directly in the center of the table sat an entire roasted pig with the customary apple within its mouth. It shared the center of the table with a perfectly roasted wild bird of some sort. Both main dishes were surrounded with several dishes filled to the rim and neatly piled up. There were plates of grilled corn, nicely steamed asparagus, accompanied with bowls of green cooked vegetables, plates of freshly baked buttery biscuits and so much more. Sitting around the table ready to enjoy this feast was an adult gentleman and an adult woman accompanied by what appeared to be their children. The adult male and woman each sat at the end of the table in their finest wares. You can clearly see that the male was wearing a dark colored fancy jacket which exposed the vest directly underneath, as well as a neatly pressed white shirt. The woman wore a very elegant two-piece velvet blue dress. The coat was neatly buttoned up exposing her figure slightly. To the right of the adult male sat an adolescent male dress in a suit jacket that resembled the adult male. Right next to him sat a young boy, who didn't wear a suit jacket but instead you could only see a perfectly starched white shirt on him. To the right of the adult woman sat a young girl which appeared a few years younger than the youngest male. She herself wore a printed flowering dress decorated with ruffles along the neckline and shoulders, typical for a young child of that age. The voice continues "***....as well as comfortably.***"

The scene immediately changes to an adult male walking toward the viewer with an adult woman accompanying him on his arm. They were wearing what appeared to be very soft and fluffy white robes, tightly wrapped around their bodies. The viewpoint of the screen changes to behind the couple as you observe them walking towards two big brown reclining chairs. As they arrive to their seats they each sat at their perspective seats and immediately reclined into their seats comfortably. As soon as they were in their comfortable position the chairs began to gently vibrate. There was not a sound heard, the only indication of the vibration was the subtle shaking of their bodies. The voice returns to add, "***For us to enjoy the benefits of so much wonderful advantages and comforts, there are a few obligations that we as citizens must complete. We all live a modern and convenient life due to those technological advantages yet we have to remember that there is one particular invention that has provided us that extra piece of mind.*** "

Another image emerges of a cobblestone building with only a frosted door, perfectly centered. There was no way of seeing the other side of the door, due to the frosting on the door as opposed to the clear glass that would normally appear on such doors. The voice returns with a little bit more resolve, "***This building and several ones like it across the country houses the infamous CK 730. This device is better known by its more popular name as the "The Catcher". This is one of many examples of how the great advancements made technically has greatly helped to improve our quality of life."*** The current scene begins to fade away as an image of a triage center begins to fade in. You immediately see rows of beds perfectly lined up in an orderly and military fashion. Some beds were occupied while others laid there empty awaiting their next occupant. The beds that were empty were made with perfect military corners with no other wrinkle that could be found across them. A few of the beds that were occupied had male soldiers catching what little sleep that they could, one or two of the soldiers were sitting up enjoying a good read and the remainder of the patients were simply played cards with their neighbor. He majority of the occupants of the room were male soldiers, the only women within the room were in the typical nurses uniform. For health reasons the shirt didn't go all the way to the ground but right below their ankles. The skirt didn't puff out like the normal fashion, instead it pleated neatly close to their body. In front of her blouse was an additional layer with the universal medical symbol of the Red Cross. They moved within the room with a sense of purpose as they moved from one patient to another, tending to their various ailments.

Over the image the voice returned. "***In the beginning of its conception the CK730 was originally designed to assist our nurses with the difficult task of diagnosing of patients and assisting on their ongoing care. Through this technology we fell upon an accidental convenience that has benefits us all, ever since.***" Another scene fades in of the frosted door from before. This time the viewpoint was zoomed back as patrons walked past with smiles on their faces as they engage in conversation. The patrons clothing moved perfectly as they moved past the door. "***Due to these advancements we are able to determine the manner in which you will depart from this world. Yet we would like to take this moment to remind you that it is important that we all do our part.***" The door appears to move closer as the walking patrons appear to disappear. "***This is a reminder as some prepare to enjoy their twenty-first year of their life. Please remember that it is your obligation to walk through these doors and complete your civic duty by reporting to the Future Center to receive your prediction. What better way to enjoy the ongoing benefits of the modern day?*** "

The door stops coming closer showing nothing but the frosted windows before it fades away to a black screen. "***This has been a reminder from the Civic Obligation Organization.*** "

The Dreaded Machine

They sat in the booth with their empty cups and glass sitting in front of them as an awkward silence lingered between them as if to drown out the noise of the diner. They finally gathered themselves and found courage in their actions as well as discussion. As Leon looked around, it finally dawned on him why such an array of characters or patrons were at *this* particular diner. The waiter returned politely asking if they needed anything else, when they shook their heads, he placed the check face down on the table. As he walked away, he plastered a smile on his face that matched the smiles of the passer-byers from earlier. It was a forced smile filled with complete remorse. He was getting tired of these sad looks so he purposely ignored the waiter's smile and his false attempt at lightening up the mood. Leon reached over to try to take a peek at the bill in a playful manner to cause a fuss from his mother, who in turn reacted accordingly. She quickly smacked his hand and swiped the bill, not giving him a chance to see the charges. They didn't say a word to each other as they got up at the same time and headed toward the register, it was almost as if they were speaking to each other telepathically. While his mother paid the bill, he took a moment to take a better account of the diner. He noticed that they were receiving glances from those within the diner. They almost appear to ask if they were on their way to The Future Center like most people dressed like them usually do. There was a mixture of sadness and pity within their eyes, it wasn't sure if it was for him or themselves. As he searched their faces, his eyes fell on a sign that simply read The Imperial Diner: Your **stop** after you visit to the very first Future Center ever established.' It was then he realized that THIS diner was placed right next to a Future Center, not any Future Center but the very first one. After a few moments, he recognized that their sadness may have been due to their own judgment passed down by the very machine he was destined to meet on this very day. Better yet, they were having a *really* bad day with; he secretly hoped it was the latter. For a moment, he felt a deep sadness come over him at the thought of all these people being aware of his appointment. He quickly snapped out of his sorrow when he realized that there was no way they could have known where this day would take him. While he was searching his thoughts, he stopped when he saw that in her drunken state, his mother wasn't very discrete about this being his 21st birthday. It was no secret that it was a civic duty to face '*The Catcher*' when you turned 21. His heart suddenly began to pound harder and faster within his chest. He began to feel his breathing shorten as his vision began to blur. He tried to discretely take a slow and steady breath and just as slowly let it out, in hopes that his mother didn't notice his actions as she turned from making her payment. To his relief, she didn't skip a beat as she walked past him and made her way back to their table so she could leave a generous tip. After leaving the tip, she turned to Leon with the biggest smile that she could muster on her face. That smile was the only thing light that broke through the gloominess of this dark diner. She wrapped her arms around him and whispered in his ears "Happy Birthday, my dear son!" and kissed him gently on the cheek, then without giving him a chance to react, she headed out the door. Leon rushed ahead of her to hold the door open. As they walked outside, she began to hum a happy little tune, almost to herself, but loud enough for him to hear.

When they got into the parking lot, they stopped and let out a huge unified sigh, each for completely different reasons. Leon, because he was quite aware of what was next and he was not looking forward to it nor was he ready. His mum, which due to the fact that she finally told her son her view on the 'The Catcher' and she felt that what was burning inside of her was finally released. She silently pointed him in the direction of the Future Center, this being the first time she actually acknowledged that the Future Center was anywhere within their vicinity. They quietly started to make their way in the direction that she indicated, as they did his mother must of made a misstep because she stumbled and almost fell, face first. Leon turned with a panicked look on his face. He let out a gasp as he asked, "Are you okay, Mum?" He reached out to help her up but she immediately smacked his hand away. She candidly said to him as she straightened herself, "Listen! I'm fine." She took a deep breath to gain her composure and shake off the embarrassment. She looked him squarely in the eyes and stated in a matter of fact voice, "Listen, this is like life, sometimes you trip but you get up and you keep moving. *You always keep moving*!" His mother's words took him so much by surprise that he took a few steps back. The determination from her tone caused him to delay as he took in her words completely. Once he took the moment to acknowledge her words they continued on their walk. He led the way as his mother followed directly behind him, secretly hoping her words of encouragement would get her son through this moment and the day. Within her face you could see a mixture of hope and sorrow as they continued on their way.

They walked to what at first glance appeared to be an abandoned brick office building. To add to that abandoned feeling it appeared to be void of any emotion and content in front of this building except for a frosted front door. There was not even a speck of trash within 10 feet of the perimeter of the entrance. 'Man!' Leon thought to himself, 'Even the dirt is afraid of coming near this place!' Just then his mother became very concerned for her son's ability to cope with the current situation, which was probably a reaction to the look on his face. She grabbed his hand as she began to giggle nervously and whispered into his ear, "Sweetie! Remember what I told you." She finished by giving his hand a squeeze for encouragement, which he quickly returned before they both let go. Allowing him to open the door and face his destiny. Suddenly everything started to sink in for him, his vision started to become doubled, accompanied with difficulty to breathe. As hard as he tried to remain calm it was that much harder for him to convince himself that everything would be okay. He was only able to give his mother a half-ass smile before actually pulling the door open. As he walked through the doors, it was everything one would expect. There was not a soul in the waiting room and it appeared to be very sterile. The empty rows of chairs appeared to go on forever. Not a single soul was in this place except for the scheduled staff who remained behind a glass protected section. The room seemed completely void of any type of dirt or life for that matter. Almost as if the germs were either completely cleaned out or they just as afraid of this place as the humans were. Despite the fact that no one would fault them for it; this fact did nothing to help him with his anxiety which was rapidly growing.

'What was I expecting?' He thought as the disappointment came over him. In a failed attempt to snap out of his anxiety, he returned to his routine of taking deep and steady breaths. 'What did I really expect to see? The neighborhood younglings and party-goers just shooting the breeze in here?' he paused as he glared forward. 'Come on, Leon!' He told himself as he tried to no avail to come to terms with his current situation. The Future Center was a place that everyone and anyone avoided at all cost. Most of the time people were brought in by some manner of force., all trying to avoid the inevitable. His mother quietly walked up behind him and placed her hand on his back, as a means to give her son some encouragement as well as some sort of physical support. She walked passed him into the sea of chairs they called the waiting room and let her son continue on without her. She didn't expect this day to be so difficult for herself yet despite her own worries she hoped that she provided him with enough strength to get through this. He forced himself to casually make his way to what appeared to be the receptionist's desk. Behind the location was a woman sitting there quietly behind a very thick glass. One could only assume that it was some sort of bullet proof glass. The receptionist herself had an overly joyous smile on her face as she sat behind the glass while the rest of the staff moved around with files in hand. The staff wore uniforms that were similar to the ones worn by the nurses that worked in the triage center. In almost a pleading manner, Leon turned back toward the waiting room for some sort of encouragement. Then he turned back to the nurse before him to gauge the level of tension. He stared at her blankly for a few moments before the receptionists finally asked, "Can I help you?" Leon just stared at her blankly. 'Really!' Leon thought to himself. 'I don't know where the hell I am, and needed directions. By the way, what is this place?' Instead of sharing this thought he handed her his credentials through the space beneath the glass, this being the only space shown within this glass without saying a word. She gracefully took his credentials and with a stern face she examined the photo and then him. Afterwards she was satisfied she reached down to a draw to her right. She walked over to a chamber to her left and place the paperwork in it.

A giggle escaped his lips as he thought her actions were a joke as he looked at the stacks of papers in the chamber but he quietly realized it wasn't when she slammed it shut. This must have been a regular occurrence because the only persons that jumped when the door slammed was Leon and his mother. The door slamming was intensified by the empty waiting room which caused the sound to echo. When she returned to him, she quickly donned her smile again and said with the most pleasant voice, "If you can kindly open the chamber and retrieve the papers that I have placed there. Please fill out each sheet to the best of your ability. Once you have completed this please place them back into the chamber and kindly return back to this window." Once she finished providing her instructions she didn't provide him any opportunity to react or provide any kind of inquiry. She simply got up and walked deeper into the office to undertake some other task. He followed her instructions and open the chamber, carefully grabbing the paperwork not to drop it and shut the chamber with more care then she took placing them there.
'Yeah,' he thought to himself, 'This is EXACTLY how I wanted to spend my birthday.'

As he approached his mother, awkwardly carry the pile of papers that he retrieved from the chamber. As he got closer to her, he forced a smile on his face. His mother sat next to him as he filled out his paperwork, assisting him only how a mother can. It took him a little over thirty minutes to complete every last one. He took special care not to make a fuss and worry her. Once he was finally done he walked back up to the chamber almost as if he was taking the walk of shame and placed it back in just as instructed. He walked back to the front desk where the receptionist was already waiting for him. She didn't even make a movement in the direction of the paperwork as if they really didn't matter. She simply smiled at him and stated, "Please follow me!" The anxiety that built within him caused him to stop for a moment. His anxiety was quickly replaced with a feeling of being completely inferior. He headed toward the right as he quietly mumbled to himself. 'I hope I didn't fill out all that paperwork for nothing.' As he glanced over at the paperwork filling the chamber. He reluctantly followed behind her. By the way she kept glancing behind it appeared that he wasn't following her close enough. She glanced back behind her one last time before she pushed open a door, quickly walked in and held the door open for him. As soon as he entered, she handed him a few damp paper towels and informed him of the following, "Once I exit the room, wipe you face with the paper towel, please save one for afterwards in case it is required." She paused to take a breath and then continued, "Once you finish wiping your face, dispose of it here." She quickly motioned to a shoot that was about ten feet behind him toward the back of the room. He didn't have a chance to even glance behind him to take a look before she continued with her instructions, "Then step up into the indention in the machine." As his eyes fell onto the machine, the magnitude of his current situation fell on him harder than anything he has felt before. It was an odd reaction to an appliance that sat innocently in a corner of the room. Any other time he would have marveled at the magnificence of the actual machine, but not today. When his eyes fell on it, he saw its appearance as a simple case. Nothing to imply that what laid beyond was the technological know-how that can accurately predict the method one would meet their end. This entire experience was becoming way too much for him to bear; he became anxious as he imagined himself pushing the receptionist so hard that she hit the ground hard and fast. He could see himself slowly walking toward the dreaded machine as he reached his hand out. He imagined the smoothness as his went from caressing it to smashing it with his bare hands. Making a hole that exposed wires, which he quickly started to pull out. The nurse cleared her throat in a loud and obvious manner, which quickly brought him back to reality. Once again she was satisfied that she had his complete attention, she stared into his eyes before continuing on with her instructions. "As you step into the body impression, let it form around you. Please do not resist. You'll see a bright light and then you will be released. Whether you determine that you require the second towel or not. Please dispose of it in the chute I showed you earlier. Your results will dispense on the side of the machine." She quickly mentioned that last bit of instructions. He found it very difficult to keep up with her instructions. Before he knew it she was pointing to the chute again. 'What just happened?' he thought to himself. She paused to see if he had any questions about the procedure. After about two seconds she stated, "Okay!" As if implying that he missed his chance to make an inquiry before she continued, "When you are done, just return to the window so we can record your prediction." With that she turned and walked out the room closing the door behind her.

She left Leon alone in the room to take it all in as well as The Catcher alone. Alone is exactly how he felt. With every breath he took the room appeared to double in size. The last time he felt this alone and isolated was at his father's funeral. Without any warning he was thrown back to that dreaded moment. He found himself in a spacious room. Yet despite the vastness of the room it felt to him as if he was in a much smaller room. This room was crowded with the bodies of mourners. He had forced so many more pleasant thoughts forward just to avoid this memory. Not on this day. Despite the fact that this room was filled with people, he still felt as if he was the only person left on the planet. He was able to pull away from that memory only to find himself back in this empty room. Just him and the Catcher. He took it all in as he absent-mindly wiped his face with one of two damp towels. Unlike the room in his memory, ***THIS*** room was not filled at all. Not a soul in sight. As he took in the room he realized that this room was as sanitized as the waiting room. The room was bright with no sign of furniture except for The Catcher. 'A chair would be nice.' He mumbled to himself. After placing the used towel in the chute as indicated earlier. 'Just in case' he mumbled. And realized that it was more like a blanket to provide some security. "Well I can't procrastinate any longer." He practically shouted. The echo was so loud that it caused him to jump at his own voice. As he headed toward the machine he let out a heavy sigh. His heart started to pound vigously within his chest. To the point where he was actually feeling physical pain and his breathing was beginning to become labored. He grasped at every trick that he knew to try to bring his anxiety under control. He forced his legs forward, the closer he got the harder it got for him to move them. He stood in front of the machine, he took it all in. He was overwhelmed with fear. 'I don't want to know how I'm going to die!' He screamed as loud as he could within his head, as he fought the urge to run out of the room. It took all his strength not to run out of that room like the coward he truly was. He took a moment to calm himself by taking a few deep breaths. He shut his eyes, took a very deep breath and took a step forward.

The moment he took that step into the indention it closed in on his body so rapidly that it forced his eyes to quickly open. Once his body was firmly secure the gel stopped for a moment. Then continued around his face, a lot more tightly than he would have preferred. Without having the option of getting out of the suction of the Catcher, he helplessly watched as the probes came out of the silhouette and held his eyes open. For fear of the sanctity of his eyes he slightly started to fight his jelly resistance with no success. 'No one ever said anything about my eyes." He thought to himself. Before he could try to pull away again a flash of light shined into each of his eyes for a few seconds and then probes quickly retracted. He was quickly released by the gel, which caused him to quickly jump back. "She didn't tell me THAT was going to happen," he stopped and thought about it as he ended with "or did she?" he murmured in a very disgruntled manner. He found it difficult but he still worked hard to regain his composure. As he waited for his verdict, he absentmindly wiped his face with the last damp towel which he managed to keep in his hand. He followed the instructions that was provided to him earlier about the disposal of the second towel as he awaited his dreaded verdict. He practically jumped out his skin when the verdict was spit out of the side of the machine. 'I must have forgotten about that part.' He thought. He took a moment to get himself together before making his way slowly over to it. His hand shook as reached out to grab it. He suddenly felt a surge of anger go through him. He balled his hands into a fist as he continued his approach. Once in front of the machine he took a moment to compose himself. Before another surge of emotion could come over him again he quickly grabbed the sheet and turned it over. His eyes became wide as he stared at the piece of paper for a few moments for what felt like forever. Suddenly out of nowhere he started to giggle. It quickly turned into an infectious laughter. Tears ran down his face. The more he laughed the more tears emerged. The tears were forming so fast that his vision became blurry to the point that he couldn't see the doorknob but he couldn't stop himself from laughing. He took a deep breath and found a moment to wipe the tears from his face and make it through the door. As soon as he passed the threshold, his laughter took over again as the tears descended his face at a rapid rate. The moment he went through the door; he began to laugh uncontrollably. The silence in the waiting room was broken by the laughter in the distance. Once she realized that the source of the laughter was her dear Leon. She quickly stood up in a panic. It was unclear if it was due to relief or concern because she couldn't tell if he was truly laughing or crying, hysterically. The staff behind the window had absolutely no reaction to him; they carried on as if nothing was happening. One could only guess that they probably have seen every type of reaction that could be imagined to one's verdict. She was uncertain if that was laughter or hysterical crying. 'My poor child!' she thought. 'The last time I heard him this upset was on that horrible, horrible day.' She could only be referencing her husband's funeral.   She became overcome with fear. It was as if her worst fears were coming true. 'Could it be that this was too much for him?' she thought. From her point of view, it appeared as if the entire experience was way too much from him. It seemed as if it has caused him to crack up.

Leon could barely see through the tears that built up in his eyes, causing his vision to become blurry. He blindly walked in the direction of his mother. It was like a child that was harmed in the playground reaching for their mothers' arm. His reaction was such a dramatic one that silent tears fell down her face as she watched him make his way toward her. With every step he took in her direction, her heart sank deeper. Her worry took complete control, the point where she wasn't even aware that tears were running down her face. A sudden and familiar clearing of the throat came from behind the glass as he was getting closer to his mother. He miraculously found himself back to the window where he first started this process. His vision was blurry as he stood before the glass. He glanced over to where he placed the paperwork and realized that it was no longer there. The nurse slipped a piece of paper under the glass. He took the slip and glanced at it. He started to giggle a little before returning the slip under the glass. He confirmed his verdict with a nod and then allowed the laughter to take over him for just a moment. He quickly regained his composure. Finally, his action stirred a response from the staff behind the glass. They simply stopped the task that they were tending to. Just to stare at poor Leon. They didn't dare make any motion toward the glass either. They dare not venture from behind the security of the glass. The receptionist simply stated "Alright sir! You're all done here." She slipped him his credentials under the glass and returned to her duties. As she walked back she kept her eyes on him in case he attempted to make his way past the glass. He simply nodded and headed toward his panicked mother ignoring her alarminess. She stood there parallelized with fear. As soon as he reached her, she let to a sigh and asked, "You okay, son?" upon hearing his mother's words he immediately broke into hysterical laughter. The laughter was so loud and profound that even the employees cautionly approached the glass, curious of what he would do next. Among them were looks of confusion and mixed with pity. Yet they were intrigued none the less.

Despite his mother's complete confusion, she was relieved to see that Leon could find laughter within him. Although she could not imagine what could be so funny. Seeing a glimpse of his mother's confusion, he made many failed attempts to explain. Once he realized that his laughter would not permit him, he simply handed her his verdict. She retrieved the slip of paper that he presented to her and read it. She stared at it for a few moments before the laughter slowly escaped her lips. The laughter quickly took over her. To the point where she was laughing so hard that she fell back into her seat. After a moment of continuous laughter shared between Leon and his mother, the receptionist returned to the glass. Mindful not to leave its security and never removing her eyes on the two of them. She called out, "is everything okay, Sir?" Leon couldn't stop laughing but his mom composed herself long enough to notice the looks from behind the glass as his mother simply explained, "This piece of paper states that he will meet his end by the means of a cigarette. This dear child is completely impossible." She reached into his inner jacket pocket and pulled out his bottle of Nicline and continued, "You see he **is** quite allergic to those damn things. That being said he deals and manages it with Nicline. Even if he did have any reaction it could never be enough to kill him. So to that I state that the bloody Catcher finally got it wrong." She continued to laugh. Despite her words, all that stood behind the glass was quite aware that since its conception the Catcher has never been wrong. Not even once. Leon and his mother finally got a hold of themselves, gathered themselves and finally took leave of the Future Center. As they walked pass the patrons trying to ignore or acknowledge the Future

Center. They would burst into laughter, unable to avoid drawing in the glances of the passerbyers. Once they got a hold of themselves, again, they headed back to the car, which was still parked behind the diner. Once they entered the car, they continued to laugh for a good fifteen minutes. After a while his mother turned and said, "See! Things aren't so bad after all." And they drove off.

True Heart

As Leon walked down the walkway, he passed by a tele store where he caught a sight of a popular moving advert. An image slowly fades in from the darkness of the screen. It was a simple image of a four story brick apartment complex. It resembled the apartment complex that he resided in. A voice emerged from the tele:

Are you ready to make the move from here to here?

Through the existing image a two story Victorian house emerges, with the typical flower garden bordering the path leading to the front stoop. After a few moments the front door opened up allowing two young children, a boy and a girl to run out dressed in their formal attire. Quickly behind them emerged an adult man and woman dressed in the same attire as the children. The four of them form the perfect family portrait formation as they smiled and began to wave through the screen. The scene fades out as a mosaic of squared images of several different shapes and sizes. Just like the family in the previous image, they were all dressed up with the perfect amount of makeup on their faces. From within the tele the voice announces:

Looking for that lifelong mate to start the phrase of your life?

Ready to start your family? Look no further.

The True Heart logo appears in the form of a heart with an arrow going through it. With the words 'TRUE HEART' in the center in bold, the image filled the entire screen.

True Heart is here to assist you.

Suddenly an image of an elegant restaurant appears on the scene. Within the filled dining room, you get a closer look at the dinner table where a gentleman is enjoying a meal while speaking with an elegantly dressed woman.

We have a hundred percent success rate. We guarantee that you will find the woman of your dreams. The love of your life is waiting for you.

An office appears with rows of desks neatly organized appears. Some of the desks were equipped with just typewriters from a decade or so ago. Although you couldn't see them close up it was obvious that the keys were circular and worn. On the other desks were the more modern cyber typewriters and oval in shape with a large back to hold the eternal tubing. A keyboard was neatly placed in front of the monitor. Sitting at each desk was either a male or female typing diligently. The voice returned one last time.

Stop on by and see if we can find you the woman that you deserve.

Fade to black.

Life Goes On

Some time had passed since Leon faced The Catcher about a month or so ago, it was common for a person to fall into a deep depression or even isolate themselves from the world after following the mandate to meet the Catcher. Not Leon. He moved on rather well one would say; it was as if that day was just a horrible prank as he carried on in his happy and joyful manner. Some of their friends were somewhat concerned with his complete adaptability after his visit but they dare not inquire, even his best mate Greg couldn't bring himself to inquire. Within the current state of this civilized society, it was looked upon as bad form to discuss one's verdict received by The Catcher, and, as humorous as he found his verdict, he dare not mention it. Due to this fact he knew that he couldn't discuss this with anyone outside of his mother. Nothing brings a mother and son together more than a shared morbid secret joke. During this time, they would frequently make their way down and take scrolls through the shopping and restaurant districts when Leon had a moment from his busy work schedule at the Department of Public Relations. It was on one of these particular trips that they came across an advertisement for one of the most popular cigarette brands. They both noticed it at the same time and immediately began to giggle in unison. After a few months of the odd and frequent girlie laughs shared between them, their friends began to tire of their behavior rather quickly and began to inquire about the private joke. At first they were reluctant to share what they found so funny but eventually they began to share. It started with a long-time friend of his mother's. The three of them were enjoying an afternoon of tea and conversation. Leon took a moment to skim through the daily newspaper when he came across an advert for an up and coming brand of cigarettes called Stanport. He folded the newspaper to show the ad and placed it on the table in full view for his mother. His mother was in the middle of taking a sip of her tea when she caught sight of the newspaper advertisement, she simply glanced at him to initiate the giggling between them. Her friend had had enough about this "inside joke" business and kindly asked, "Do you care to share?" her tone was one of a mother losing her patience with a young child. It was unclear if it was the question or her tone that caused them to immediately quiet their giggling. His mother didn't know how to respond to her. It was Leon's prediction after all so she simply glanced in her son's direction. It was unclear why he nodded at his mother, giving her his approval to proceed. She let out a sigh, yet it was unsure out of relief or anxiety but she proceeded to explain Leon's encounter with The Catcher a few months ago. When his mother's friend first heard the story she found it odd and didn't believe them until they showed her his slip. After examining the paper, she began to laugh hysterically, finally getting the joke. After this encounter, they slowly started to open up to their closest friends about their secret jokes. They were all aware of Leon's deadly allergies to cigarette as well as his meticulous efforts taken to avoid them and manage it. It was all in the Nicline. Leon took daily doses of his Nicline just to be able to tolerate the accidental run in with the daily tobacco smoker. Finally, their friends were able to share in their girlie giggles but within their giggles they secretly hoped in their hearts that their own predictions could be just as wrong. But they never shared this wish. Leon selected his friends especially for the reason that they didn't partake in the action of smoking. Once they got to know him they took special care not to bring any who did near him as well. They knew better than to even come near him if they were around someone who would leave a hint of cigarettes on them. This was always done as a precautionary measure because one never knew when he consumed his latest dosage or if he would have an episode despite of it. Although it wouldn't lead to his death at that particular moment, it would lead to a long and painful stay at the hospital for him.

As time went on and with his secret being known to his closest friends he became a bite more relaxed and oddly confident. This was the time that a fair young lady caught the attention of Leon by the name of Juliette Quesetine. It took him completely off guard, when he was on one of his strolls among the shops. That is when she caught his eye, as he strolled on the opposite side of the street taking in the shop windows. There she was casually strolling down the walk as she carried her recently purchased items. The sight of her made his heart jump up with joy, there was no way he was going to let this beauty get away. He quickly but casually made his way across the busy street. As he approached her, he removed his hat and gracefully bowed. "Kind lady," he stated nervously as he paused to catch his breath before continuing. "May I have the pleasure of assisting you with your bags?" he was trying to contain his excitement as he spoke. She immediately began to blush as she bashfully nodded. Her perfectly rosy cheeks added that much color to her fair face and big bright green eyes that almost shined like one of those rare stones found at the jewelers. Her hair was pinned up in a fashion that barely allowed it to pass her shoulders, allowing her deep dark brown hair to shine in the sunlight.

As they stood side by side it was obvious that she was about half an inch shorter than him. She was obviously a full figured woman which was very appealing to Leon. She was so pleasant and lovely that she just didn't win his heart but his mother's as well. Juliette and Leon spent a lot of their free time together, when that wasn't possible they chatted over their mobile phones. After being courted for a time, Leon felt that it was time to ask her out on an official outing. This had to be really special, so he decided to take her out on a trip to a natural preserve just west of the city. The government set aside land that could never be used for further development. It was a nice way for citizens to take a break from the hustle and bustle of the city. It was perfect for some quality getting to know each other time. Since Leon didn't own his own vehicle, he borrowed his mothers'. It took them about an hour to drive to the secluded location. They enjoyed the scenery as they shared tidbits of their week. After their hour long drive, he jumped out of the vehicle and ran to the other side to open the door for her exit. After she took in the surroundings, he quickly grabbed the picnic basket that his mother had gracefully put together for them by his mum. Once it had been secured he gracefully offered Juliette his arm and off they went down one of many worn paths. They leisurely made their way up the trail to take in all of nature. They wondered at the different variety of flower, with their brilliant colors and shapes. When they weren't in awe of the botanicals, their eyes went to the skies. In awe, they watched the unique and exotic birds that had either taken shelter among the trees or stretching their wings within the skies. They took in the wonderful views as they made their way to their romantic picnic. This was the first of many wonderful and romantic dates that they had. With the time that they spent together, it was not long before he finally was introduced to her parents. To Leon's wonderful surprise they resided only a few blocks away from the home he grew up in and where his mother currently resided in. He was surprised that he had never known of them before. He wanted to make a wonderful impression on them so he dressed in his finest attire, outside of the suit he would wear to attend his mate's weddings. Which was beginning to become a command affair. His attire was fancy but not too fancy; he wore a dark blue ruffle shirt accompanied with a pair of black slacks and a matching coat jacket. He simply added a squared off top hat to finish of his ensemble as he escorted Juliette to her parents' home. As they made their way down her parent's walkway his nerves began to go into overdrive. He worked really hard to control his breathing as his legs suddenly felt like Jell-O sticks. 'It must be because I don't know them.' He thought. 'Get a hold of yourself mate! What's the worst that can happen?' When they finally arrived at the door, he took a deep and obvious breath. One that he couldn't nor did he try to hide from her. She simply squeezed his arm before knocking on the door. They were greeted by her father who adorned a smile on his face from ear to ear. Right behind was his wife, elegantly glowing with happiness. With a welcome like that he began to immediately relax and actually enjoyed the company with her parents. During a very homely dinner they enjoyed conversation about the state of the government, the war and anything that could be found in the daily papers. After that dinner, Juliette and Leon spent equal time between both parent's home, and the majority of their free time together. They were inseparable. After being by each other's side for four years he decided that it was time to seal the deal with her and make her an honest woman. Aside from saving for the traditional months to purchase the ring of his choice, he spent months with a personal jewelry designer to create the perfect ring to finally ask her for her hand in marriage. He planned every detail perfectly, right down to where and when he would pop the question. He decided that the best time to ask her would be during the annual 'Coming out of summer' bash before all their friends and mates. His best mate Gary graciously hosted the event every year on the top of his apartment complex. Their friendship however had become quite strained since Leon has met Juliette. From time to time they would run into each other, spending a brief moment catching up before continuing on their journey. They no longer engaged with their regular outings to the gentleman's pub. With the absence of Leon in his life Greg had taken up the awful habit of smoking with his new mates. He also showed no desire to settle and resign from the single life. This new habit was his way of punishing his best friend for choosing to end their bachelorhood going-on with all its fun and games to settle down...with *her*. Since he met Juliette, he no longer went on their normal outings to the gentle men's pub and he saw less and less of him as time passed.

Leon's nerves grew as the big day approached, he found it hard to keep his composure when he was anywhere near Juliette. He stumbled over his words and feet as if it was the first time that they were dating. The week before the bash Juliette decided that they should have a nice romantic dinner together at her cottage, which was in a community for young ladies going through their own adulthood transition. The cottage sat on half an acre of land and was a one - bedroom cottage equipped with a full kitchen and bathroom. She answered the door and practically took Leon's breath away. The majority of her hair was in a bun except for a few strands that hung down on her face, which framed her stunning smile. She wore a chiffon blue formed gown with sleeves of lace with a matching blue. The gown was low enough to cover her ankles. Since she wasn't going anywhere, head attire was not required. She prepared a nice three course meal for the both of them. They started out the dinner with a nice light green salad; it was light to make room for a perfectly baked rump roast with a side of grilled asparagus and golden roasted potatoes. She finished it off with a delicately baked mousse. They laughed and talked as if they were on their first date. They started to reminisce on their first date, Juliette immediately went to the flowers she saw along the path "Oh!" she started "Do you remember those beautiful pink and purple star flowers? They were so lovely especially how they lined the path." They continued on talking and reminiscing about all the other sights and sounds they experienced. They also remarked how surprisingly short their trip was up the path. They giggled about how nervous Leon was and it showed when he ate so slowly in fear that he might spill his food in front of her. They also joked about how she cut up her meal into tiny little bites so she didn't disgust him while they were eating. After they had their fill with dinner, they decided to spend a romantic moment on her coach, which was plain but cozy enough for the two of them. It must have been their trip down memory lane because they couldn't keep their hands off each other. It was almost as if they were reliving their first date again, like before it was just the two of them among nature. There couldn't be more of a mood breaker than when Juliette suddenly sat up with her back more rigid that an old solid tree. Once she was sitting up she began to stare straight into his eyes, it wasn't really intended to be a romantic look and it didn't have that effect on him, which alarmed him as heart began to pound fast and hard within his chest. It was more like a look of deep concern that came over her face, which alarmed him. 'Did I do something wrong?' he thought to himself. 'Did I offend her? I can't make her mad at me so close to the party. Not now!' Her eyes showed that she had a heavy burden to share with him as well as her nervousness caused her eyes to shake uncontrollably. She took a deep and dramatic breath and blurted it out. "Leon," she paused for a moment to let the words form on her lips. "I'm pregnant!" It took him about 30 seconds for the shock of her words to settle in. 'What did she say?' He thought to himself, and suddenly a feeling of joy, confusion and anxiety began to overwhelm him. He was so overwhelmed that almost completely forgot what he had planned for next week. He has been holding on to the ring for a little bite. 'I have been holding on to it for a while now.' He thought to himself and realized that now was better than later. Without speaking a word to her of acknowledgment, he shot up and quickly made his way to her room where he had placed his belongings earlier upon his arrival. All she heard from her bedroom was rustling as he searched frantically for something she could only guess, after a few moments of the rustling sound he finally emerged with his hand behind his back. He has played this moment in his head over and over, never did he picture this moment going this way. His head was swimming with excitement and so many ideas. 'I really didn't intend for it to happen like this.' He thought to himself as he left the room. Yet with such great news there was no better time. As he caught sight of her, he immediately began to sweat as his legs began to shake so bad it was almost difficult for him to walk. All the while he was looking squarely into Juliette's eyes even from a distance. When he finally was in front of her, he could see the confusion and fear in her face. He took a deep breath and dropped onto one knee as she froze in shock. He presented her with a closed velvet blue ring box. Her mouth dropped as he opened the box and presented her with a blue emerald stone in the center, cut in a rectangular shape that was about .31 carat cut in the classic emerald cut. The emerald was surrounded by miniature circular diamonds, all sitting on a shiny gold band. This was a surreal moment for both of them. With tears streaming down her face, she heard Leon ask. "Juliette Quesetine, we have spent the last four years together and my life has been all the better for it. I can't see my life without you in it. What I'm trying to say?" he paused to swallow. "What I'm trying to ask you is... Will you do me the honor of becoming my wife?" They both pause to take in the moment. 'Wow! What a night of full of surprises!' They both thought to themselves. The emotions between them swelled so much inside both of them that it filled the room. It didn't take long for the emotions began to spill over to their exterior, before either of them could realize tears were falling from their eyes. Leon became a bite more anxious from a lack of a response from her, while a frog developed in her throat filled with emotion. She could barely get out the word she so desperately wanted to scream out. After a few moments she finally managed a ... "Yes!" She managed to say as she fell to down on both her knees besides him. They embraced in celebration of their wonderful evening and union. They were so excited that they couldn't wait to tell their parents. Before heading out they checked the time and decided that it was too late, and they would do them a favor and notify them tomorrow. They savored the moment and each other for the night.

First order of business the next day was to inform their parents, so they invited his mother out to brunch to a restaurant that he and Juliette frequented through the years. She was quite aware that Leon was going to propose and even helped him choose the ring. They agreed to all meet at the restaurant instead of the house. As they greeted each she was surprised to see Juliette wearing the ring a week earlier than her son had discussed with her. Leon smirked to himself when he saw the look of confusion on her face when she glanced down at Juliette's hand, he wanted her to stew and wonder for the moment. The joys a son will have on his mother's behalf. She wondered why Leon changed his timetable and neglected to inform her. She pondered on what could have caused him to propose so early. 'Well these young ins now a days have no patience.' She thought to herself. 'He probably couldn't wait any longer. I really don't know why. It was only a week away.' Despite her curiosity she didn't say a word; she enjoyed the service at the restaurant and the meal. She was going to let them inform her of Leon's reason for the sudden change of plans in their own time. When they finished their dessert and Leon paid the bill, he decided that as soon as they left the restaurant he would finally announce to her his good news. 'She has stewed long enough.' He thought to himself. As they exited the restaurant he grabbed his mother's hand and stated. "Mum! We have good news!" She looked at them with a smirk as she glanced at Juliette's hand as she responded. "I already know dear. I was just wondering when you were going to let me in on the big secret." She knew that this was not the plan that Leon discussed with her but she understood that he was young and probably couldn't wait any longer. She was so excited that she didn't give either of them a chance to respond before she added. "I am overjoyed that you two are finally getting married and I am going to be a mother in law. I always wanted a daughter, even if she will be my daughter in law. I will love her just the same." She stated as she walked ahead of them in a playful manner. Leon stopped and stated. "That's not it Mum. Juliette is pregnant." She stopped dead in her tracks and looked at them with a blank stare. 'What did he say?' She thought before she turned around. With a reaction like that one can clearly see the fruit doesn't fall far from the tree, as one would say. Then an overwhelming feeling of joy came over her face. She suddenly howled so loud that she took Leon and the passersby which she didn't even acknowledge. Right after her shriek, she ran back to them and grabbed both Leon and Juliette as she pulled them in for a tight hug. Finally, she managed to make an audible sound that sounded like a shriek and then cried out. "Oh my God! What GREAT news! You have just made me the happiest woman on earth." She paused for a moment to take hold of her emotions. "This universe." She was so happy that it took her a few moments to realize that she was out in public as she broke out in dance in the middle of the street. A few people that walked by just glanced at them oddly for her behavior in public. "I knew he was the one from the moment I met him." Juliette stated while his mother paid the glances any mind.

They spent the rest of the afternoon walking around town giggling while planning a wedding and a baby shower. This wasn't how Leon wanted either announcement to be made; he wanted to wait until the party to announce their joyous news to everyone. Juliette couldn't wait to tell everyone. After escorting Leon's mother home, they made their way towards Juliette's parents' home to share their announcement with them. Her father was aware of the upcoming proposal because Leon did do the honorable thing and ask for his permission before hand. However, her mother was unaware and pleasantly surprised with the announcement of their engagement. She completely lost her composure with the news of the pregnancy and the fact that she was actually going to be a grandmother. Despite her joy, there was a sadness in her eyes. Her father, not so much so, but he didn't let his disappointment ruin his wife's joy. Everyone was so excited that they didn't know where to begin with the planning of a wedding and the new arrival. The weeks leading up to the party was filled with nothing but joy for both Leon and Juliette. It was as if she was walking through her very own fairy tale. One thing for sure is that she wanted to get married no later than 3 months from the day of the party, because she didn't want to show as she walked down the aisle and it was not in proper form of a lady.

Nicline

Leon's mother sat in front of the tellie as she enjoyed a cup of tea. The screen filled with white dots dancing about. From this image a living image of an elegant gentleman's lounge filled with elegantly designed chairs and table. Within every chair was seated well-dressed men of high society. The room was filled with plenty of smoke. Every other gentleman either had a cigar or cigarette in hand. Everyone was engaged in conversation while sipping their drink of choice. The announcer's voice emerges from the scene.

Do you find it difficult to partake in intellectual conversation or even socialize within society all due to your allergies to tobacco and nicotine?

From within the image of the gentleman's lounge an image fades in of a busy cobblestone street, filled with bustling vehicles and patrons going on their daily errands and task. Among this busy street fancy shops line the sidewalk. In front of every shop are large glass windows designed elegantly to showcase their particular specialty. The view changes to the angle of a person strolling down the busy street.

The view shook as if you are the person actually walking down the street, which caused the view not to appear as stable as the previous scenes. As the man makes his way down the sidewalk you notice passer byers walking from every direction. Every woman that passes into view flashes a bashful smile occasionally accompanied with the pleasantly shy giggle before continuing on their way. After passing a few women, two gentlemen come into view engaging in conversation. As they get closer, it becomes apparent they both are enjoying lit cigarettes. As they lift it up to take a drag the scene freezes.

Would this situation send you into a panic due to your own unpredictable allergies to tobacco?

An image fades in of a woman dressed in the cocktail uniform from one of those upper class waiting establishments. The uniform was basically black in color with white borders. The skirt was proper as it was floor length. It was trimmed with white that appeared like an apron. Her dress did expose some of her cleavage but only provided an acceptable amount of exposure. She wore a pleasant smile on her face as she held a dark bottle with a white label on it. The image slowly becomes bigger until it's the only thing that fills up the screen and the woman is completely out of view. As the picture gets closer you could see the label clearly. In dark letters you see the words **Nicline.**

Fear no longer. Nicline is here to ease your allergies and assist you in becoming more socially comfortable as well as acceptable!

A scene appears within a movie house. You are looking into the audience, when a gentleman catches your attention as he pulls out a cigarette and proceeds to light it. The gentleman directly behind him reaches into his inner jacket pocket and pulls out a little bottle that you can see the Nicline logo. He puts on a smile and states:

I have no worries. Thanks to Nicline.

Another scene appears of a gentleman walking with a young lady in the park engaged in pleasant conversation. As they walked, they encountered another couple and immediately engage in conversation. As they talk the voice emerges again.

There is no reason to leave your home in fear due to your nicotine or tobacco allergies. Trust in Nicline to aide you in becoming an active part of society again.

There is a moment of silence as the scene continues during the disclaimer voices over.

This product may cause spontaneous nosebleeds, shortness of breath, nerve pain, uncontrollable bowel movements, skeletal breakage and insomnia. Should you feel any of these side effects please notify your physician immediately.

The scene fades to black and the scene turns off.

Summer Bash

When the night of the bash arrived, they both were so excited. They giggled and danced around like children on Christmas Day. They were so excited that they couldn't wait to get there. Once they finally arrived, they socialized with a few of their friends they haven't seen in years and some they just saw the other day. All before making their way to the rooftop. Some of those that they spoke with immediately noticed the engagement ring on her finger and suspected that there were nuptials in the future. Yet, they didn't inquire nor appeared too inquisitive or rude. As they interacted among their friends, they continued to behave as if they had just started dating. They were constantly glancing over to each other with bashful eyes accompanied with a smile. The actual bash was held on the roof of Gary's complex and has become an annual occurrence, so the entire complex participated. Their celebration was actually an extension of the festivities. As they made their way up to the roof, they ran into a few of Leon's running mates and took a few moments to catch up on what has changed each other's life. They were overjoyed with his news of the engagement and their expected new arrival. Upon the roof, the couple discovered a small section filled with cigarette smoke and in the center of all that smoke stood Gary. He finally decided to make his way to Gary to have a quick chit-chat. Gary was upset with the man that used to be his best mate but this wasn't the time to sort out differences. So he forced a fake smile on his face and made a whole hearted effort to sound cheerful as he greeted Leon and Juliette. "Hey guys! I am so happy you could make it." He maintained the proper manners as he took a moment to bow deeply in front of Juliette and gently kissed her hand before straightening up and continued with his commentary. "It seems like forever since I have graced your presence." He directed his words to both of them. "What have you two birdies been up to?" he tried to maintain his fake smile and some interest. Leon ignored his falseness and continued in his famous cheerful manner, he wasn't going to let his old mate ruin this night for him. "Well it's wonderful seeing you, too! We wouldn't miss this for the world. As usual, you are the most gracious host and this is a wonderful bash." Leon stopped for a moment to let out a cough from being overwhelmed by the building smoke. "We actually have some wonderful news to share with you..." He stopped mid-sentence to let out a cough to clear his throat. "... and everyone else." He started to cough again as he grabbed Juliette's hand to display her ring. "We're getting married. I finally have the chance and honor to make an honest woman out of her. Especially now that we're expecting!" Leon ended with a cough as his eyes were beginning to blur and the coughing started, he held Juliette closer more for strength than for a show of endearment. He knew the physical implication that this was having on him but he was more concern on what this was doing to their unborn child, especially not knowing if the child has his affliction or not. By this time, the smoke had spread throughout the entire rooftop, and there was no safe place for him up there. Both Juliette and Leon made their way back down to the street so he could breathe a little better. That much tobacco smoke was starting to make his current dosage of Nicline quite ineffective. Once they finally made it down to the actual street, the fresh air cleared out Leon's lungs. As they stepped out, they ran into an old friend of Leon's that he hasn't seen since Juliette has entered his life. His long time mate, Joseph was attending the bash with his current companion, Brittany. Joseph use to accompany Leon and Greg on their many boyish outings. "Leon!" he exclaimed, excitedly "How are you? It's been more than five years since I have seen you!" he mentioned as they shook hands and shared pleasantries with the women. As the chatted Leon felt his symptoms subside as it became a little bit easier as they joked around and caught up.

While Joseph and Leon caught up on the street, Greg agonized over the encounter that he just had with Leon, as he smoked one cigarette after another. He lit the latest cigarette and realized how much he truly did miss Leon and their friendship. He realized that his actions had helped bring a divide between them. In deep thought, he suddenly became highly upset with his current behavior. He wished he had more time to talk to his old mate or would have behaved in a more appropriate manner. Outside of his rude and childish behavior, he was quite aware that his new smoking habit, as well as his new friends that partake took, was high health risk for Leon. He started to contemplate the current status of their relationship. 'I have to talk to him. We have to fix our friendship. I know we can fix this.' He thought to himself, completely unaware of Leon's exact location below him. 'Maybe I should give this up and see how I can fix the current situation' he thought to himself as he eyed his lit cigarette. Without giving it a second thought, he flicked his cigarette off the roof. Meanwhile, directly below him Leon was giggling with tears in his eyes as Joseph was telling him their boyish jokes as the ladies held their own conversation. "So she looked him squarely in the eyes and said 'Sir, I am NOT one of your whores and smacked him so hard that she left her hand print, bright and red on his cheek." As Joseph finished his joke, no one could have imaged what happened next. Leon threw his head back in laughter. Leon's mouth opened wide as the cigarette that Greg flicked off the roof fell slowly down toward the street. As if in slow motion, it found its way right down into Leon's throat. Everything happened so fast that it took a few moments before anyone had any idea what had occurred or what was truly going on to react.

Besides the burning feeling in Leon's' throat, he wasn't aware that his throat was starting to close up. He started to feel an intense itching take over his entire body then he felt light headiness and a sensation of falling. At first, they thought he was choking from his own laughter but Leon began to go through a violent allergic reaction. He gasped to get some air as his throat closed up quickly, he then began to shake violently and fell to the ground. His face quickly became covered with dark red hives. "OH MY GOD!" Juliette yelled. From that moment life slowed down for all. She ran to catch him, to help him as quickly as she could, but he was dead before he hit the ground.

Jobba and Doma

A black screen appears on the television as Gary sat there drinking his sixth glass of whiskey. He watched as the screen gave way to people sitting in rows of chairs. Almost everyone was weeping.

In this day and age death isn't so much as a surprise as it used to be but it doesn't make the pain that much less.

From the image a brick building emerges. The sign above the door made it look like an average office. A sign greeted all that looked at the building, simply stating: **'Jobba and Doma: Funeral Services'**

Here at Jobba and Doma, we use every resource at our disposal to assist you in providing a respectable farewell to your dearly departed loved ones.

This particular room was filled with different types of coffins. They ranged in different styles from a plain pine box to a completely gold and perfectly polished. It appears to be the showroom.

We understand how much your departed meant to you. And we have an array of choices for you to provide the proper final resting place for your beloved.

An eloquently designed couch emerges, with a middle age

woman sitting in deep thought as she sipped a hot cup of tea. While she was sitting, two well-dressed men walk up to her with paper in hand stopping to give a brief explanation and went back on their way.

We are with you every step of the way. You don't have to go through this alone.

The image of the establishment fades in again.

Let us help you in your time of grief.

The scene fades out.

The Funeral

Juliette didn't know what to do with herself; she was having trouble comprehending what had occurred before her. She just stood in front of Leon's mother's house as the tears streamed down her face uncontrollably. 'How am I supposed to tell her?' she thought as she stood there with her legs shaking so bad that she truly didn't know how she was still standing. She couldn't find the strength to lift her arm and knock on the door. 'We were laughing about how impossible this could be just two days ago.' She thought to herself as she forced her arm up to finally knock on the door. She replayed the conversation in her head. They were sitting at her dining table when Leon reached into his inner pocket and pulled out his latest bottle of Nicline. She immediately began to giggle. "With this..." She reached for the bottle. "We know that The Catcher, can be wrong." Leon began to laugh as he replied, "And for that we are very fortunate." And he leaned over and kissed her. The memory of the conversation faded, and, she finally knocked on the door. As soon as his mother answered the door she knew something was wrong. Her facial expression went from her usual cheerful disposition to urgent concern to complete denial as she searched for Leon behind Juliette. She opened her mouth several times to ask the question but she was terrified to know the answe. She finally found the courage after a few moments of silence. "Juliette, where's Leon?" she asked as she held her heart in her mouth. Juliette began sobbing uncontrollably as soon as she heard the question. Leon's mother hushed her more in an instinctual manner than anything else as she led her into the house. After a few moments you could hear from behind the door a woman scream. '***NO!***'

Two days had passed since that fateful night at the party. The devastation that filled the room was beyond words. The grief was so great that no one knew what to do or say. The entire room was decorated in black and tears, accompanied with sides of puffy eyes. There were very few words heard between the constant weeping. The attendees were both local and from afar and every single one of them were inconsolable. All to pay respect to a most beloved Leon. Everyone that attended the Summer Bash was in attendance, as a form of respect the smokers left their cigarettes at home. All except for Gary, who remained outside lighting one after another. He put his cigarettes down long enough to step inside for the ceremony and pay his respects. As he stepped in the reeking stench of cigarettes announced his presence before he was seen. As the stench hit the mourners, they paused in shock. When they caught sight of him they stopped in their tracks and stared at him. They didn't make any attempt to hide the hate and disdain towards him. This was from smokers and non-smokers alike. He was definitely not welcomed there; the grim reaper would have received a warmer greeting. He couldn't believe that he smoked the actual cigarette that killed his best mate. It was killing him knowing that his intention for that cigarette was supposed to be his last one. As he walked through the room, it was obvious that everyone present was aware that it was his cigarette that killed Leon. This didn't help ease his guilt and only made it worse because he was ready to fix their broken friendship.

The entire memorial was long and very emotional. The atmosphere was filled with people weeping and wailing from all corners of the room. Leon's mother hadn't stopped crying since the moment she heard the news. Her face was mucked and flooded with tears. She was completely stricken by grief; no longer was the classic cheery smile. She realized the time had come to bid her son a final farewell. She wiped away her tears and finally made her way to the casket. Her only son. Her only baby is gone. Since learning of her son's death, she hasn't spoken audibly due to all of the tears. She was so weak in the knees that she stumbled a few times. Eventually, it became obvious that she needed the assistance of the others to make it to the coffin. She stood silently in front of her son's casket and silently cried over her son. After a few moments, she reached into her inner pocket and pulled out a piece of paper and stared at it for a moment. It resembled the one that he received on his twenty-first birthday from The Catcher. She placed it on Leon's chest and kissed him on the cheek and attempted to walk away but stumbled. . Curiosity got the best of a gentleman nearby who witnessed her actions. He reached for the paper and read it. A look of concern came across his face as he turned in time to see her collapse to the ground sobbing uncontrollably.

Made in the USA
Middletown, DE
09 February 2022